The Sparrow and the Mustard Seed

written by

Dr. E Sebastian Bolden

illustrated by

Jalonnee M Moore

For more information about Universal Inspirations LLC
or to order online, please visit **Universalinspirations.com**

Tellwell Talent
www.tellwell.ca

ISBN
978-1-77370-657-3 (Hardcover)
978-1-77370-656-6 (Paperback)

Photography by February Photography

Dr. Errol Sebastian Bolden is a full professor and owner of Universal Inspirations LLC. Although this is his first children's book, he has authored several inspirational books and other creative works. A native of Barbados in the Caribbean, Dr. Bolden currently resides in Baltimore, Maryland and frequently travels throughout the Caribbean and Africa. Grounded by his Christian faith, The Sparrow and the Mustard Seed highlights Christian principles manifested through a child-like spirit and love. His literary style is eclectic and several of his writings have an Afrocentric focus. He attends New Shiloh Baptist Church in Baltimore, Maryland. Dr. Bolden is a Maryland Responder and a certified grief recovery specialist.

My Creative Writings

Previously self-published books:

The Journey of the Heart

Feeding the Spirit: A Book of Prayers and Personal Reflections

The Journey of the Soul

Standing Still: A Devotional Guide for Black Males

Coming soon:

Tabansi and the Golden Touch

Tabansi and the Golden Touch Professional
Development and Leadership Guide

The Lord is My Shephard: My Journey into His Presence

The Fabric of a Liberated Soul

The Final Journey: Questions, Issues
and Concerns during one period of Transition

Summary

The book *The Sparrow and the Mustard Seed* is a children's book that tells a story that persons of all ages can relate to: love, joy, comfort, and protection. Parents, guardians, baby sitters, teachers or anyone who may be reading this story with or for a child(ren) will be encouraged by reading it. It celebrates the beauty of family and more importantly, intergenerational relationships. The main character Crystal, with her childlike innocence and curiosity, absolutely cherishes spending time with her grandparents and enjoys conversations with her dad. Even as she misses her grandfather's physical presence, she finds joy in knowing that he is well taken care of. The story also portrays the father in the role of nurturer, a role too seldom celebrated by or expected of fathers. The dad helps his daughter get through the first major loss of her life in way that is light-hearted, and relevant for children. Finally, in a way that only a little child could, she comforts and challenges her grandmother to have faith. This is a family book for children and parents with illustrations that are joyful but relevant.

Acknowledgement

I would like to acknowledge the support of several persons who made this book possible. First, I would like to thank my God who is the source my strength and comfort. I would also like to thank my dear friend Kreis Mattox whose late night conversations with me about how he engaged his children in a difficult discussion about a health challenge he was encountering, served as the impetus for this book. Thank you Kreis! To my friends Dr. MiUndrae Prince and Mr. Kerry Belgrave, thank you for your editorial, and conceptual feedback, as well as your encouragement. Finally, I would like to thank my colleagues, Drs. Shirley Newton-Guest, and Mary Wanza. Thank you for your confidence in the relevance of my work and your ongoing support.

Dedication

This book is written to all children who are part of my sphere of influence, particularly my oldest goddaughter Richelle Thompson and my other godchildren, nephews and nieces. It is also written to all children who may be dealing with the loss a loved one or who themselves may be experiencing a less than desirable situation that may be causing them some pain or sadness. This book is also written for fathers who celebrate moments with their children. It seeks to provide comfort through the awareness that God, as a heavenly father, cares and is looking out for and after all of us.

Grandparents are special. This is a lesson that little Crystal learned early in life. She was her grandparents' pride and joy. To them she could do little wrong, and every morning they were delighted to have her parents drop her off so they could babysit her. They had toys of every kind for her and even built a special playground for their first grandchild. They were always bought clothes for her and enjoyed dressing her up like a doll.

Her grandfather loved to carry her on his shoulders and would tickle her with his beard. He would also take her to the park to play and feed the pigeons. Her grandmother loved to let her play dress up with her clothes, wigs, and Sunday morning hats. She was the only one her grandmother allowed to wear her Sunday church clothes. She would also sing and read with her. Crystal was always smiling and hugging them, for she loved them so much. Her grandparents loved each other very much and seemed inseparable, often finishing each other's sentences.

Crystal was four years old when she started preschool. Although her grandparents were a little sad that they would not be spending as much time with her now that she will be going to school, they were happy because going to school would allow Crystal an opportunity to meet children from different backgrounds at the school she would be attending. A month before she was about the start school, her parents and grandparents started preparing her for the experience. They told her of the new things she would learn, the new children she would meet, and the games she would play.

Crystal was so excited the night before she was to start school she could barely sleep. As she entered the school, she was happy but nervous; and she cried a little when her parents first dropped her off. However, that quickly changed as she saw all the children on the playground. From her first day, she got to learn of the different places where the other children were from. And just as her parents and grandparents told her, she got to play new games which were her favorite thing to do.

After her first day at preschool school, Crystal hurried home to tell her grandparents how much fun she had at school. She talked about her teacher, her classmates, and, of course, recess and all the new games she learned how to play. She even wanted to teach them how to play some of the games. As excited as she was about her first day, she ended the conversation by saying, "I had fun at school today grandma and grandpa, but I missed you more."

Over the next couple of years, Crystal continued to enjoy school very much. She really loved playing with children from different backgrounds and learning different things about them. Two of her three best friends were children from different countries, and she enjoyed having them sleep over. Her family also enjoyed cooking for them and watching them all play together.

One day after school, something happened that was new for Crystal. She witnessed her grandfather's sudden illness and soon after his death. She was so sad and had so many questions. She wanted to know why her grandfather left her alone. Some of her questions were: Does he not miss her and grandma? Who is taking care of him? Will he ever come back? Why did he have to leave?

The sparkle in Crystal's eyes began to slowly disappear. Shortly after her grandpa died, Crystal noticed that there was a beautiful little bird that started building a nest outside of her window. The bird would sing as it built the nest. Crystal began to look forward to the bird's visit. Much to her surprise, she later found out that a bird had been building a nest outside of her grandmother's bedroom as well.

One morning, shortly after Crystal's mother left for work, her dad noticed that she was a little sad. He approached her, and gave her a hug and asked, "What's wrong?" Holding her head down she whispered, "I miss grandpa," and a tear rolled down her cheek. Softly kissing her forehead, her dad said, "Come let me tell you about the sparrow and the mustard seed."

Lifting his daughter unto his lap, Crystal's father began talking to her. "Crystal, the little bird that builds the nest outside of your window is called a sparrow. This little bird represents care, attention, happiness and the building of a home or a nest. The sparrow also looks for food, and protects its young. "Does this remind you of anyone, Crystal?" She responded, "That is Grandpa." "You are right," her dad said. "Grandpa did these things for me and for your uncles and taught us how to do them. He knew that there would come a time when he would have to go away, and I would have to do them for my children so they could have a full and happy life." "Isn't that hard work daddy?" Crystal asked. "Who looks after you when you have to work so hard?" "God does, baby," her dad replied. "He puts persons in our lives like mom and other family and friends so that we can take care of each other. That is what God's love does."

Smiling and lovingly pinching her cheek, her dad continued talking with Crystal. "The other lesson I need you to know about the sparrow is that even though the sparrow has to work hard all year looking for food, building a home and protecting its young, it does not suffer because God looks out for the sparrow. He keeps His eye on the sparrow so that the thunder and the lightning, the heat, or the cold would not be harmful to it". Crystal clapped her hands and shouted, "Yeah, yeah!" She was so excited that such a little bird could be that strong and caring. Her dad looked at her and chuckled before continuing. "What you need to know my little princess is that even as God looks out for the sparrow, He looks out for us, His children, even more. So, He is looking out for us, and He is looking after Grandpa." Crystal then asked her dad a series of questions:

"But daddy, how can I know for sure?" "Does every father look after his child?" "No baby," her daddy replied, "but that's where faith comes in. We have to have faith." "What's faith, daddy?" Crystal asked. "Faith is something that you cannot see but you know it is there. You cannot see the wind, but you see things moving because of the wind. Or when you see a chair, you sit on it because you have faith that it is strong enough to not break when you sit on it," her dad replied. Crystal continued with her questions. "How much of it do I have to have for things to be good?" Her dad responded by sharing another story. Let me tell you another story. This one is about a mustard seed. "What is a mustard seed daddy?" Crystal asked while tugging on her dad's shirt. "Patience, Princess," he encouraged.

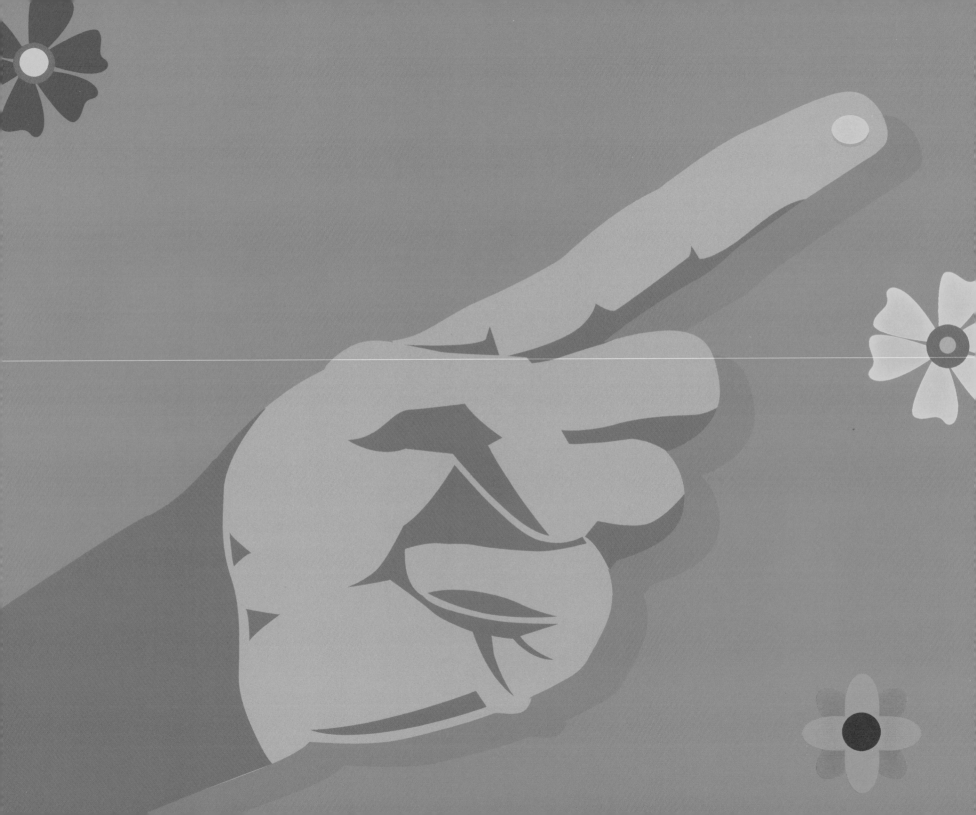

Now Crystal's dad loved gardening. He grew fruits and vegetables and various plants for spices to cook food. Mustard was one of those plants he grew for spices. They walked through the garden to find a mustard plant that had a pod with seeds. Finding one, Crystal's dad picked a pod with seeds and carefully opening it, he took out a mustard seed and placed it on his index finger and asked, "What do you think baby girl?" She responded, "It's tiny daddy," "Exactly Crystal," her dad responded, and then he proceeded to tell her about the mustard seed.

"The mustard seed is a tiny seed that is used as a spice. It is one of the tiniest seeds found in places in the Middle East such as Israel, Egypt and Saudi Arabia but can produce a big tree," her daddy shared. Crystal asked with a puzzled look on her face, "Really daddy?" "Yes sweetheart," he replied. He then shared the message from the Bible found in *Matthew* 17:20 when Jesus told the disciples that if they had faith as small as a grain of mustard seed, they could say to the mountain move and it would move. Crystal asked with child-like curiosity, "Do you mean that all of the big rocks and trees would just move if I tell them to?"

"It is a little more to it than that baby," her daddy said. "Tell me daddy, tell me!" she said excitedly. Finding a smooth rock in his garden, he sat her on his lap and patiently explained. "What it means, my little princess, is that it only takes a little bit of faith to do big things, just like it takes a little mustard seed to grow into a big tree. We just must have a little faith in God so that He can do big things for us just like taking care of grandpa and all the others who are now in Heaven, and those of us here on earth. What we have to do is to trust and have faith in Him. We have to believe Him when He says that He will always take care of us. That is what trust is all about Crystal. It is believing that He will do what He says He will do."

"I have faith in Him, daddy!" Crystal declared. Her dad kissed her and said, "I know, baby; I know. "As they got up to walk back towards the house, Crystal held her dad's hand and stopped as she turned to him and said, "Daddy, I love the stories about the sparrow and the mustard seed. Thanks daddy!"

A few weeks later, on a beautiful sunny Saturday morning, Crystal joined her grandmother for a trip to a nearby park as they sometimes did. On this day, her grandma seemed a little quieter than usual although she did get more excited when she greeted her granddaughter and received a special hug. As they walked to the park, Crystal noticed a beautiful brightly colored sparrow fly pass her and rested on a bench near to the spot where they were walking.

She then held her grandmother's hand. As they sat, Crystal turned to her grandma and said, "Grandma, do you see that sparrow?" She shared with much excitement, "God is looking out for the sparrow just like He is taking care of grandpa". She then held her grandmother's hand and told her the story of the mustard seed as well. After she had finished sharing with her grandmother the story about the mustard seed, she said to her grandma, "You will be okay, just like grandpa is okay; you just have to have faith!" Crystal then asked in her high-pitched voice, "Grandma, do you need a mustard seed?" Grandma smiled.

Thanks for reading!

CPSIA information can be obtained at www.ICGtesting.com
Printed in the USA
BVIW12n0749170918
527365BV00011B/30